Show and Tell

Featuring Jim Henson's Sesame Street Muppets

by Patricia Relf
Illustrated by Tom Cooke

A SESAME STREET/GOLDEN PRESS BOOK
Published by Western Publishing Company, Inc.
in conjunction with Children's Television Workshop.

It was Show and Tell Day at school. Everyone
brought something special to show to the class
during Show and Tell time. Betty Lou hid hers in her
cubby hole.

Bert put a big box in his cubby. He wouldn't tell
anyone what was inside. "I want it to be a surprise,"
he said.

"Come on, Bert," said Betty Lou. "Let's help
Herry." Herry Monster was building a block castle.
Nearby, Grover was reading a book and Ernie
was making a clay animal.

Soon everyone gathered around the teacher.

"Psst, Betty Lou!" Bert whispered. "Is it Show and Tell time?"

"Not yet, Bert," said Betty Lou. "It's story time."

Bert had trouble keeping his mind on the story
the teacher read to the class. He was thinking about
his Show and Tell surprise.

After the story, everyone sat down at a table.
"Oh, boy," Bert said. "Now it's Show and Tell time!"
"No, Bert," Betty Lou said. "Now it's time to
paint."
Bert was disappointed, but Betty Lou loved to
paint. She made a picture of a beautiful bird.

When they were finished,
they washed their hands and put
their paints away. Bert cleaned up
faster than anyone else.

At last everyone was ready for Show and Tell.
Bert could hardly wait for his turn.

Cookie Monster was first. He had brought his
cookie cutter collection. He had large cookie cutters
and small cookie cutters; he had square cookie cutters
and round cookie cutters. He had Gingerbread Man,
Santa Claus, and Easter Bunny cookie cutters.

Rodeo Rosie showed the class the lariat
that her cousin Duane had brought her from
Oklahoma. She could rope almost anything
with that lariat.

Josie showed the class her new roller skates and skated in a figure eight.

Ernie paraded around the classroom to a marching beat that he played on his drum.

Grover and Prairie Dawn had made a tin-can telephone from cans and string. Prairie Dawn held the tin can to her ear, and Grover spoke into the other end.

"Hi, Prairie Dawn," he said into the can. "It is I, lovable furry old Grover."

"I can hear you, Grover," answered Prairie Dawn.

Farley showed everyone the rubber-band airplane he had made. The airplane flew from one end of the room to the other.

Herry Monster had brought his
dancing shoes for Show and Tell.
He demonstrated a leap that he had
learned in dancing class.

Jamie went to his cubby hole to get what he had brought. It was a large pumpkin that he had helped his mother to grow.

At last it was Bert's turn. He hurried to his cubby to get his surprise for Show and Tell.

But when Bert opened the box, it was empty! "Oh, no!" he wailed. "I brought a special surprise to share with you for Show and Tell — Bernice, my pet pigeon. But now she's gone, gone, *gone*!"

When they saw the empty box, they all began
to look for Bernice.

"Don't worry, Bert. We'll find her," Betty Lou
said. "Look! Pigeon tracks!" Sure enough, Bernice
had walked across the wet paintings and left footprints
all over the room!

Betty Lou followed the tracks along the art table...
across the bookshelf... and into the play area.

"Ssh!" said Betty Lou, "I think I know where Bernice is!"

She crept up to Herry's block castle... lifted up a block from the roof... and out flew Bernice!

"Bernice!" Bert cried, holding his arms out to her.

"Hey, she liked my castle," said Herry Monster.

"Catch her!" everyone yelled.

But Bernice was scared by all the noise. She flew all around the room and no one could reach her.

Finally Bernice landed on a high shelf.

"We'll never get her down!" cried Bert.

"Wait a minute!" Betty Lou said. "I think it's time for me to bring out the surprise *I* brought for Show and Tell."

"Show and Tell? At a time like *this?*" Bert moaned.

But Betty Lou was already opening her package. "It's peanut butter raisin bread that I made myself," she said proudly. "Be quiet, everybody, and let me try something."

Betty Lou sliced off a piece of bread
and crumbled it onto the floor. She
made a path of crumbs that led straight
into Bernice's box.

Bernice saw the crumbs. She looked
at them for what seemed like a very
long time. Finally she hopped down from
the shelf and started eating. Following
the trail of crumbs, she ate and ate until
she ate her way right back to her box.

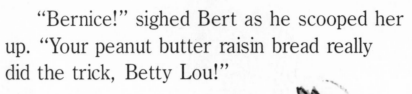

"Bernice!" sighed Bert as he scooped her up. "Your peanut butter raisin bread really did the trick, Betty Lou!"

"How about a piece for you, Bert?" asked Betty Lou. "And the next time we have Show and Tell, why don't you leave Bernice at home and bring your bottle cap collection instead?"